Talking Snakes

It was Lucy's first day at Hargraves
Juniors. She didn't know anything.
And she didn't know any*one*, except
for Harriet.

Lucy looked around. Mum had said
that in summer girls could wear red-
checked dresses or blue-checked dresses.
Lucy was wearing a red-checked dress.

All the other girls were wearing
blue-checked dresses.

A teacher came to the door
and blew a whistle. Everyone
else lined up neatly. Lucy had
to be pushed into place by
some older girls.

Harriet laughed.

It was better when they were in the classroom. Mrs McAfee said nice things about Lucy's drawing.

Lucy pointed to India on a map.

But then
came lunch.

Lucy sat alone.

Harriet had lots
of girls at her table.
But Harriet didn't ask Lucy to
sit with her. And Lucy didn't want
to sit with Harriet anyway.

10

After lunch was playtime. The boys
played football. The girls did skipping.

Lucy went over to where the girls
were skipping. A girl with a nice smile
asked if she would like a turn. But
Harriet said loudly, "Lucy can't skip."

So Lucy
walked away.

The bit of the playground under the
trees had paving-stones. Lucy was
looking down at the paving-stones
when Mrs McAfee
came over.

Mrs McAfee had
brought Lucy a
wooden box full of
coloured chalks.

"Here," Mrs McAfee
said. "You can use
these if you want."

First Lucy drew
a giraffe, with a
long yellow neck
and big brown eyes.

Then she drew
a golden lion with a
fluffy orange mane.

When she had finished the lion,
it seemed to look at her. It even
seemed to speak. But the bell rang
and Lucy couldn't hear what it said.

14

Lucy wasn't the only one
not playing. Two of the new boys
didn't play football – Zack had terrible
asthma and Ibrahim got too hot.
They sat on a bench all lunchtime.

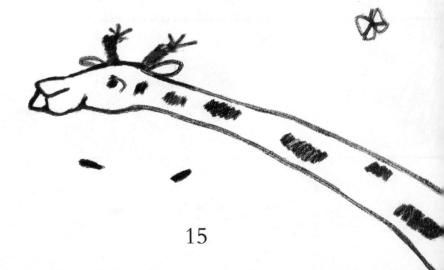

Zack sat on one end. Ibrahim sat
on the other end. They didn't talk to
each other. But they both watched
Lucy drawing.

Lucy hadn't noticed them.

The next playtime, Lucy drew again.
Ibrahim and Zack sat on a bench very
close by. They watched again.

Lucy drew a brown monkey
with stone-coloured face and hands.
"That's very good," the lion said.

Lucy looked at Ibrahim and Zack.
Then she said, very quietly,
to the lion, "Thank you."

"No," the monkey
said. "Thank *you*.
What a lovely day.
I like it here. I can see all
the way up this tree."

The boys on the bench didn't
seem to have heard.

Very quietly, Lucy said, "I'm glad
you like it."

Then the bell rang.

19

The third day, Lucy drew a long
yellow snake. The tail went almost
under Ibrahim and Zack's bench.
The snake had a thick neck, big
black eyes and a pointed mouth.
The pointed mouth screamed when
Lucy put down her chalk.
"Aaaaagh!" it said.
"It hurts, it hurts!"

Out loud, Lucy asked the lion, "What's wrong with him?"

She had forgotten about Ibrahim and Zack.

"If that's a python," Ibrahim said, "it should be greener."

"Pythons are only that yellow when they're poorly," explained the lion.

"Oh, no!" Lucy said. "There isn't time to colour him green."

Ibrahim got down off the bench. "I'll help," he said. "You can break the chalk in two."

"Break it in three," Zack said. "I'll help too."

22

Lucy did the head,
Ibrahim did the tail
and Zack did the
middle bit.

They finished
just as the bell went. "Ah," the snake
said, "that's better. Tell the boys
I'm very glad they helped."

Lucy was putting the chalks away.

She said, "Thanks so much for helping."

"You're welcome," Ibrahim said.

Zack only smiled.

But as they lined up, Zack whispered to Lucy, "What are we going to draw tomorrow?"

Talking
Elephants

25

It was Lucy's second week at
Hargraves Juniors. For the first week all
the girls had worn blue-checked dresses.
Lucy had been the only one in red.
But Lucy's mum had gone shopping.
Now Lucy wore a blue-checked dress.

All the other girls wore red-checked
dresses.

Harriet thought it was very funny.
All lunchtime she laughed at Lucy.

Lucy was sitting with Ibrahim and Zack. Ibrahim had a huge lunch with lots of sweets and pastries. His mum was a baker. He shared the sweets with Lucy and Zack.

Lucy took a bright green ball and bit
into it. It was the sweetest thing she
had ever eaten. It made chocolate seem
savoury.

Zack couldn't eat any because
it might have nuts in.

That morning Mrs McAfee had told
them about Noah's ark.
All the animals had been
two by two.

When they went out to play,
they looked at the animals they
had drawn last week.

There were a giraffe,
a lion, a monkey and
a snake that Lucy had
done on her own.

And then there was
a very large elephant that
they'd all done together.

Zack said, "They
ought to be two by two."
"That's a good idea,"
Lucy said.
"Me first!" all the
animals shouted.

"We should do the
giraffe first. It's a herd
animal," Ibrahim said.
The giraffe smiled.

"I think I'll do a lady
lion," Lucy said.

Ibrahim was already working
on the giraffe.

Zack thought the monkey
was too hard. He thought he
could do an elephant on his
own if it was little.

They worked all through
playtime.

The next morning the
weather was cool. On cool
summer mornings students
could wear the school blazer
or the school cardigan.
Lucy wore the blazer.
Everyone else was
wearing the cardigan.

Everyone except Ibrahim and Zack.
They hadn't talked about it – it just
happened. Ibrahim couldn't find
a cardigan to fit him.
Wool made Zack itch.
And Lucy's mum
thought blazers
were smarter.

During morning lessons, Mrs McAfee said it was nice to see girls and boys playing together. She said she would like some girls to try football this playtime, and some boys to try skipping.

After lunch there was a lot of
giggling at the other end of the
playground. But Lucy, Zack and
Ibrahim didn't notice. They were
working on making all the animals
two by two.

Lucy had finished her lady lion and
was working on another monkey. Zack
was helping. And Ibrahim was doing a
lady elephant. He hadn't seen Zack's
small elephant in the shade.

By the time Zack noticed, it was too late. They had three elephants.

"We could rub yours out," Ibrahim said.

"Oh, no! My baby!" the lady elephant cried.

"We can't do that," Lucy said.
They were about to get cross.
Just then, the snake shouted,
"Look out!"

They all looked. A ball
was coming very fast,
right for Zack's head.

Lucy pulled Zack's arm, hard.
Zack fell onto Ibrahim. The ball
went into the shrubs.

Harriet came after it. She looked hot
and sweaty. "Oh, *sorry*,"
she said. But she wasn't.
She got the ball.
Then, as she walked by,
she kicked the wooden
box of chalks.

Chalks went
everywhere.

The three friends had to
work fast. They had to get all
the chalks back into the box
before the bell rang. But the
animals helped.

"I have a brown one on my finger," the monkey shouted.

"I can see the red in the roots of the tree," the lion said.

The boys didn't answer the animals. And even though Ibrahim got the brown chalk and Zack got the red chalk, Lucy wasn't sure they'd heard.

But as the bell rang she saw
Zack pat the snake's head.
"Thanks," he whispered.

Talking Up
a Storm

In the third week, everyone had a
best friend. Lucy didn't know how it had
happened. On Friday no one had a best
friend, but by Monday, everyone did.

Harriet's best friend was Mandy.
Mrs McAfee let them sit together for
lessons. They ate together at lunch.
They played together at playtime.
All the girls had best friends.
All the boys had best mates, too.

Only three people didn't have
a best friend – Lucy, Zack and
Ibrahim.

At playtime they drew a lady snake.
They didn't talk much. They were all
thinking about the best friend problem.

Lucy thought if she *had*
to have a best friend,
it should be Ibrahim.
Ibrahim knew so much
about animals.

Ibrahim thought
if he *had* to have a
best mate, it should
be Zack. At least
Zack was a boy.

Zack thought if he
had to have a best mate,
it should be Lucy.
Lucy was so much fun.

49

As they made the last
marks with their chalks, the snake
spoke. He said, "Thank you for my
friend. She is beautiful."

"Ooooh," the
new lady snake said.
"Cheeky!"

Lucy, Zack and Ibrahim
looked at each
other and
laughed.

Then the bell rang.

The next day, Lucy brought Ibrahim
in a videotape. It was a programme
on pythons from the Discovery
Channel. Ibrahim didn't get
the Discovery Channel.

Lucy tried to ask Ibrahim to be her
best friend, but Ibrahim wasn't listening.

Ibrahim was getting a little white paper box out of his bag. He gave it to Zack. He said, "My mum made these specially. No nuts at all, no nut traces."

Ibrahim tried to ask Zack to be his best friend, but Zack wasn't listening.

53

Zack was getting a box of
watercolour pencils out of his bag.
He gave it to Lucy. He said, "My
mum doesn't use these any more."

Zack tried to ask Lucy to be his best
friend. But Lucy wasn't listening either.

They thought about it all morning.
Lucy felt bad that
Ibrahim didn't
notice her.

Ibrahim felt bad
because Zack didn't
notice him.

And Zack felt bad
because Lucy didn't
notice *him*.

55

Lunch was just as bad. Lucy kept
trying to talk
to Ibrahim.

Ibrahim kept trying to talk to Zack.

And Zack kept trying to talk to Lucy.

By playtime, no one
was talking at all.

"Why all the
long faces?"
asked the
lion.

Lucy looked at Ibrahim.
Ibrahim looked at Zack.
Zack looked back at Lucy.

Lucy said, "Everyone has
a best friend. Except for us."
"Oh," the lion said.
"Oh," the snake said.
"Oh," the monkey said.

All the other
animals just nodded.

Ibrahim and
Zack nodded too.

For a moment nobody said anything. The wind blew through the big tree. Leaves fell onto the monkey, the lion and the snake. Lucy, Ibrahim and Zack brushed them away.

"You know," the lady elephant said. "There are three of us, too…"

"That's true," Lucy said.

"The elephants were meant to be two by two. But there are three of them."

"Of course," the lion said. "You don't have to be just two best friends."

"We could be three best friends," Lucy said.

She started to smile. Zack and Ibrahim smiled too.

Just then, the wind blew
very hard. Many more leaves
fell down onto the paving-stones.
Then rain began to fall as well.

"Inside, everyone!" called Mrs
McAfee. "Hurry!"

Once they were in the classroom,
Mrs McAfee came over to
where they stood.

"I suppose you three
want to sit together
too," she said.

"Please, Mrs McAfee,"
they said at the same time.

She showed them a new table by
the window. They went to move
their things.

Outdoors, the paving-stone
animals were washing away.

But only Mrs McAfee noticed.

Lucy, Ibrahim and Zack were too
busy talking.